普通高等教育"十一五"国家级规划教材
2007年度普通高等教育精品教材
（高职高专教育）

# CENTURY BUSINESS ENGLISH

# 世纪商务英语

## 口语教程
### （专业篇Ⅰ）（第二版）

新世纪高职高专教材编委会组编

总主编 刘杰英　主　编 王瑛　朱巍娟
副主编 许静　刘燕华

大连理工大学出版社

**图书在版编目(CIP)数据**

世纪商务英语口语教程.专业篇.1/王瑛,朱巍娟主编.—2版.—大连:大连理工大学出版社,2007.8
普通高等教育"十一五"国家级规划教材
ISBN 978-7-5611-2940-1

Ⅰ.世… Ⅱ.①王…②朱… Ⅲ.商务–英语–口语–高等学校:技术学校–教材 Ⅳ.H319.9

中国版本图书馆 CIP 数据核字(2007)第 127234 号

大连理工大学出版社出版

地址:大连市软件园路 80 号　　　　　　　邮政编码:116023
发行:0411-84708842　邮购:0411-84703636　传真:0411-84701466
E-mail:dutp@dutp.cn　　　　　　URL:http://www.dutp.cn
大连理工印刷有限公司印刷　　　　　大连理工大学出版社发行

幅面尺寸:185mm×260mm　　印张:5.5　字数:110 千字
附件:光盘一张　　　　　　　　印数:21001~27000
2004 年 9 月第 1 版　　　　　　2007 年 8 月第 2 版
2007 年 8 月第 3 次印刷

责任编辑:李　岩　　　　　　　责任校对:史　光
　　　　　　　封面设计:波　朗

ISBN 978-7-5611-2940-1　　　　　定价:22.50 元

# 总序

　　《世纪商务英语》是新世纪高职高专教材编委会富有积极的进取精神的一次大胆尝试。

　　由大连理工大学出版社组织推动的新世纪高职高专教材编委会，是一个由全国100余所志同道合的优秀高职高专院校组成的高职高专教材建设者联盟。编委会走过的历程，见证了我们的与众不同：编委会是迄今为止第一个完全按照市场原则来长期进行高职高专教材建设运作的大型组织。从编委会诞生的第一天起，我们就选择了以高职高专教材的特色建设为己任。这不仅是由于我们拥有对高职高专教育未来发展的更为贴近实际的认识，也由于我们拥有一整套完全属于自己的切实可行的关于教材建设的创新理念、创新组织形式与创新运作方式，更由于我们一直以来对高职高专教材品牌、特色与创新的始终如一的执著追求和坚忍不拔的长期努力。

　　在编委会的所有经历中，关于教材建设理念的独到解释非常值得一提。这一理念可简述如下：所谓教材建设，就是建立在教学实践基础上的教材的不断深化、不断完善的过程。在编委会的整个教材建设过程中，这一理念不仅已成为我们的核心指导原则，而且它的深受高职高专教学单位欢迎的结果，也鼓舞了我们实现任何高职高专教材特色建设的勇气。

　　然而，高职高专英语教材特色建设的情形则有所不同。就其实用性而言，高职高专与非高职高专的英语教育并无本质区别，加之我国高职高专教育发展的历史尚短，高职高专英语优秀人才的累积也略显不足，因而，许多早期高职高专英语教材的编写，宁可倚重非高职高专院校的英语教师参与，有其积极的意义。但是，按照我们教材建设的上述理念，如果不能以高职高专一线教师为主体来实施高职高专英语教材建设的具体运作，就根本无法实现完全适合高职高专教学需要的英语教材建设预期。

　　这的确是一个两难选择。事实上，编委会要建设自己品牌的高职高专英语教材的想法由来已久。但我们也深知完全依靠一直很少涉足英语教材建设的高职高专一线教师来完成这一重任的艰难程度。因此，我们并没有从一开始就贸然地启动这个项目，而是选择在较好地实现了足够数量的非英语类高职高专教材特色建设的经验累积，若干专业英语类相关教材建设的成功尝试，以及对公共英语相关项目的具有积极意义的探索和准备之后，才开始尝试涉足这个领域的。

　　尽管我们在推进高职高专英语教材建设的过程中遇到了诸多困难，但终能如愿以偿，在很大程度上也有赖于我们的一些具有重要指导意义的体悟。编委会有一句名言：我们相信用心与努力胜过相信经验与资历。编委会有一个信条：在目标一致基础上达成的共识优于任何情况下的一己之见。这些在非英语类高职高专教材建设中屡试不爽的成功做法，在高职高专英语教材建设的过程中也得到了同样的印证。

我们欣喜地看到：由于我们付出的辛勤努力，我们的关于教材建设的上述理念，也正在英语教材建设中显现其非凡魅力。在我们高职高专一线教师所立足的英语教学实践这个基础之上，由我们自己培育出来的一株幼苗正在茁壮成长。我们现在或许还不能做到足够完美，但是，我们始终坚信：我们会比任何人都更加清楚地知道自己需要什么，只要我们坚定不移地朝着既定目标不懈努力，就一定会越做越好。

我们已经跨越了起跑线。我们绝不会放松前进的脚步。我们正在推出的包括《综合教程》、《听说教程》、《口语教程》与《阅读教程》在内的高职高专商务英语系列教材——《世纪商务英语》必将伴随着赞誉的鼓励与批评的鞭策，日臻完善，走向成熟。

耕耘过后，我们期待着在一个有足够创新精神的编委会的土壤里成长出更多更优秀的高职高专商务英语教育人才，期待着收获一个更好更切合高职高专商务英语教学实际的教材品牌。

新世纪高职高专教材编委会
2004 年 6 月

## 序

　　全球化首先表现为经济全球化,而全球化面临的一个重大障碍就是语言交流的障碍。全球化大环境下的中国又处于经济全面对外开放的形势下,这就更加激起了外语学习的热潮。如果说在我国改革开放初期国家主要需要的是专门学习外语的人才,那么在经济全球化的今日,需要与外国人打交道的就远远不止是专门的外语人才,而是各行各业各个层次的有关人员。如果说传统的涉外活动多涉及外交和少数对外贸易的垄断部门,今天则是全民从事涉外活动,而首当其冲的全面涉外活动就是与外国人做生意。这不仅涉及传统的进出口的大公司,连农民个体生产者要出口自己的产品也要进行涉外交易。就连旅游点的当地老乡也会拿着自家的小产品向外国游客兜售。所以满足涉外贸易需要的"商务英语"(Business English)就成为全民涉外活动的第一语言需要。

　　这种"商务英语"与传统的"商务英语"既有共性又有差别。相同之处是都属于专门用途英语(English for Specific Purposes),是共核英语基础的延伸。不同之处在于今天的商务英语的使用者是各行各业的全民,其中既包含传统的商务英语的使用者,更涵盖对英语一知半解却又需要使用英语进行各自的"商务"活动的人们。后者已经是或即将成为这一群体的主体。

　　这一更为广泛的商务英语的使用群体需要学习什么样的英语呢?传统的先打好英语语言基础再学习与商务活动相关的专业英语的思路显然是与此要求南辕北辙的。十几年来我有机会受教育部的委托从事高职高专英语教学的研究和指导工作,与高职高专教育英语课程教学指导委员会一道探索出了"实用英语"这一高职高专英语教学的大方向,受到了教育部和全社会的肯定和欢迎。据此我认为,我们今天提供给读者的"商务英语"应该体现如下理念:

　　1. 职业教育的重要组成部分:"商务英语"是我国职业教育的重要组成部分,其教学目标首先是培养实际使用英语去从事涉外商务活动的能力,也即能够处理商务业务的"实用英语"。

　　2. 符合各个层次的实际需要:这一需要不是学会一门外语的需要,而是学会使用英语去从事实际涉外交际的需要。换句话说,学习目的不是为了今天或以后学会一门外语,而是为了实际涉外交际的迫切需要;

　　3. 学一点、会一点、用一点:不把外语作为一门语言来学,更不作为一门学问来学,而要作为一门技艺来学。不强调打下厚实的语言基础,而突出实际技能的培养。

　　4. 口头交际和书面交际:涉外交际首先要突出听说交际,文字书面交际只是口头交际的支持和凭证。或者说,初级交际更要突出口头交际,高级交际才涉及书面交际的强有力的支持。因此教学安排要先听说后阅读,以改变我国外语教学以教授阅读为主的思路。

　　5. 教学内容要有针对性:首先要以市场需求和就业为导向,这也就是我上面所说的"实用英语"。不过"实用"本身还是一个宽泛的概念,"实用"还要有针对性。既要针对市场需求,又要针对培养人才的类型和所要达到的培养目标。同样培养酒店涉外服务人才,经理和服务员的培养要求是不同的,因此其学习内容的针对性既会有共同的实用性,更会涉及不同岗位的差异性。但在强调针对性差异的同时,还必须寻求针对性中的共性才能避免英语教学走上个性化教学的极端。

因此,编写商务英语教材首先要对其使用对象进行定位,找出其需求的共性和差异,而后再针对共性照顾差异地去编写相应的教材。《世纪商务英语》的使用对象首先是高职高专商务英语专业的学生,其次是使用英语从事涉外商务活动的广大商务工作者。他们具有以下共性:

1. 他们都在中学学过一定程度的英语,打下了初步的英语基础;

2. 他们学习英语的主要目的是使用英语去从事各自的业务活动;所涉及的涉外活动首先是口头涉外活动,其次是业务中需要处理的商务文献,如商务广告和业务单据等。

3. 他们需要学英语,但学英语又不是他们的主要目的。因此他们没有足够的时间去打扎实的语言基础。他们学习英语的主要目的是为了利用英语从事商务交际,收到学习英语的"即期效果"。

基于以上考虑,《世纪商务英语》的编者遵循了如下编写原则和思路:

1. 分层次有针对性地体现"实用":《世纪商务英语》分为通用涉外交际、通用商务交际和外贸实务交际3个层次,其中通用涉外交际又包含日常涉外交际。也就是说,《世纪商务英语》涵盖涉外商务活动的各个层面,既涉及基础英语,又涉及商务业务英语,力求将二者紧密结合融为一体。既从基础学起,又渗透实用场景下的语言交际。与此同时,《世纪商务英语》还为特定的涉外英语交际技能的培养编写了诸如商务写作、商务阅读、函电与单证等教程。

2. 重视听说、加强表达、突出实用阅读:教材编排以听说训练为主导,引导学生获取表达技能,实现课堂教学的"学一点、用一点"的原则。阅读则突出实用性文献资料,寓文化教育于实用教学之中。

3. "精讲多练"、"讲为练"、"练为用":教材不只是"教",更要注重"学",不是"教懂/学懂",而是要"教会/学会"。

4. 选材注重涉外语言交际的典型性、实用性、思想性、时代感、趣味性、可模拟性和可操作性。这样教材才能保证"教起来生动,学起来有趣,便于模仿,学了能用"。

《世纪商务英语》是在体现"实用英语"这一职业英语教育大方向的改革实践中迈出的新的可喜的一步。尽管会有这样那样的不足,但其认真探索职业英语教育的努力是值得充分肯定的。我相信,《世纪商务英语》一定会受到大家的爱护和欢迎。

孔庆炎

2007.1

# 前言

　　《世纪商务英语——口语教程》(第二版)是普通高等教育"十一五"国家级规划教材,是新世纪高职高专教材编委会组编的商务英语类课程规划教材之一。这是一套由高职高专商务英语教学一线的优秀骨干教师为主体编写的高职高专商务英语口语教材,旨在最大限度地适应高职高专学生英语基础与培养目标的要求,努力缩小高职高专商务英语教材与商务英语教学中存在的差距。

　　为了进一步将高职高专英语课程倡导"学一点,会一点,会一点,用一点"的教学指导思想贯彻到教材编写中,实现"实用为主,够用为度"的教学目标,突出学生的主体作用,调动学生的学习兴趣,循序渐进地培养学生的英语交际能力,我们对这套教材进行了修订,删除了陈旧话题,重新选材,梳理章节内容。

　　《世纪商务英语——口语教程》(第二版)在第一版基础上做了如下修订,使其既保留原有特色又具有新的特点:

## 1. 思路创新

　　本系列教程的一、二册独立成册,三、四册以一家出口公司要打开国外新市场为主线,从市场调研开始到参加展销会、接洽客户,经过各项交易环节最后达成交易,同时还涉及了一些相关的后续服务内容。内容连贯、完整,各单元的情景对话紧扣主题,语言简单、明了、地道,练习与课文联系密切,围绕课文中的关键字、词、句进行训练,具有较强的实用性和针对性。

## 2. 内容时尚

　　话题包括日常生活片段、学生从入学到毕业求职的整个成长过程,以及各种交际场合和各种商务活动;商务内容涵盖营销策略、企业文化、市场竞争、风险投资,客户服务等各个方面。话题力求时尚,且有助于学生做好初到职场的知识技能上的铺垫和心理上的准备,充分体现实用、够用的原则。

## 3. 模块新颖

　　本系列教程打破了传统的思维定式,参照国外同类英语教材,按照"图片导入—情景对话—强化训练"的顺序构建教材的框架体系。这种"表达优先"的创新设计,易于调动学生的学习兴趣,激发学生的自主表达愿望。

## 4. 层次分明,梯度明显

　　《世纪商务英语——口语教程》(第二版)从第一册到第四册有梯度,有层次,在难度上不断提高,同样在每一课中也体现出层次的要求,力求使学生学完本系列教程后可以用英语进行商务交流。

## 5. 可操作性强

　　练习多样、选材真实、指示简单明确,具有可操作性。练习环环相扣、逐层递进、由浅入深、抓住关键、反复操练,有利于学生在接近真实的轻松语言环境中,不知不觉地脱口而出,表达自己的思想感情,完成交际目的。

　　《世纪商务英语——口语教程》(第二版)共分四册。一、二册为基础篇,三、四册为专业篇。第一册是实用英语,以生活口语话题为主,以场所为主线;第二册是交际英语,逐渐渗入商务话题,以活动为主线;第三册、第四册是专业英语,引入商务业务话题,以商务活动及业务流程为主线。

《世纪商务英语——口语教程》(第二版)每册教材包含12个单元,每单元由4个模块组成。包括:

**1. 热身(Warming Up)** 这一部分以图片导入,引出关键词或提出小问题。让学生做些小练习,主要目的是通过新颖、有趣的活动,积极地调动学生大脑信息库中已经储存的有关话题的背景知识或词汇,从而激发学生主动开口说英语的能动性。

**2. 情景对话(Situational Dialogues)** 这一部分向学生提供两到三个情景对话,前后呼应,难度逐步加大。内容新颖、主题明确、表达贴切、时尚,并突出重点句型和词汇的练习。目的是训练学生的口语感知能力及模仿能力,同时为后面的练习提供参照依据。

**3. 练习(Practice)** 这部分内容是本系列教程的重点,也是其特色之所在。练习分为四个部分,难度逐渐加大。从简单的词、句模仿到开口编对话,让学生从不敢说不会说到敢说会说,从一句话到一段话,再到一个完整的对话,循序渐进地训练口语能力。

Practice1是句式语言点训练, 目的是强调学习重点, 让学生模仿和记忆。Practice2是拓展练习,即在第一个练习的基础上适当进行句式、表达方式的训练,即在模仿和记忆的基础上进行表达练习。Practice3是个 free talk,即设计场景,让学生根据前面课文及第一、二个练习中掌握的表达基础编对话,自由发挥,形式多样,如 pair work、role-play、discussion、group work、etc.。Practice 4 是对学生掌握知识的提升和课后拓展,需要学生在课后花点时间和精力去做,第三、四册基本做成 presentation 的形式,训练学生的综合素质,考核学生的综合表达能力。

**4. 多学一点(Learning More)** 这一部分内容充实,与课文主题有关。从第三、四册开始相应增加后续练习,目的是向学生介绍一些与本单元主题有关的背景文化知识等,作为前面几个模块的必要补充。教师可以根据课堂教学需要选择利用这些材料,也可以作为学生的课外阅读材料,以此拓宽知识面,适应今后工作的需要。

本系列教程每册参考学时为30~60学时,各院校在实际教学过程中,可根据具体情况对教材内容作适当增删。

本系列教程由广西国际商务职业技术学院刘杰英负责统筹,任总主编。

《世纪商务英语——口语教程 专业篇Ⅰ》(第二版)由王瑛、朱巍娟任主编,许静、刘燕华任副主编。

教材中如存在纰漏之处,敬请各相关高职高专院校和读者在使用本教程的过程中给予指正,并将改进意见及时反馈给我们,以便下次修订时完善。

所有意见、建议请寄往:gzjckfb@163.com
联系电话:0411-84707604

编　者
2007 年 3 月

# Contents

| Unit | Topic | Page |
|---|---|---|
| Unit 1 | Market Research | 1~6 |
| Unit 2 | Market Analysis | 7~14 |
| Unit 3 | Sales Promotion | 15~20 |
| Unit 4 | Advertising | 21~26 |
| Unit 5 | Trade Fair | 27~32 |
| Unit 6 | Brand Power | 33~38 |
| Unit 7 | Corporation Introduction | 39~45 |
| Unit 8 | Invitation | 47~52 |
| Unit 9 | Visiting a Plant | 53~58 |
| Unit 10 | Making an Inquiry | 59~64 |
| Unit 11 | Making an Offer | 65~70 |
| Unit 12 | Price Reduction | 71~76 |

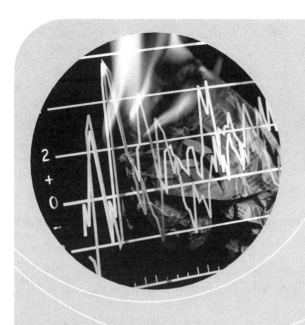

# Unit 1

## Market Research

# Warming Up

**Business people use market research very often to gather information around their business.**

(a) Brainstorm with your partner and make a list of the information which is important to know about the other countries for an Import and Export company.

Information list:

1. tax policies and regulations
2.
3.
4.
5.
6.

(b) Where can the company get the information needed? Please make another list of information sources.

Information sources:

1. newspaper
2.
3.
4.
5.
6.

# Situational Dialogues

## Dialogue 1

Li Yan, sales manager in Boyi Arts Trading Company. Zhang Jian, marketing manager in Boyi Arts Trading Company.

*Now Li Yan is asking Zhang Jian for some advice on how to carry out a market research.*

**L:** Well, Mr. Zhang, how do we start selling our corn basket to a new overseas market? Do the salesmen just walk into the customers' premises[1] and say, "Here is a wonderful new thing from China."?

**Z:** Well, from marketing point of view, it pays to do a lot of market research before you can sell anything to your customers.

**L:** How is market research carried out?

**Z:** That's a very wide question indeed. Whole books are written on this subject. But first of all I think you should do some exploratory research[2] to get a feel of your market.

**L:** Can you specify what sort of information I should look for?

**Z:** First of all you've got to find out if there's any demand for our new product, and what sort of competition we will meet. Then there are local legislations and preferences. Take packing material for example, some countries don't allow hay or straw, in case they contain bugs.

**L:** But where can I get the information I need?

**Z:** For a start, from embassies and consulates, chambers of commerce and trade associations, local trade magazines and customs import and export lists.

**L:** It seems to be a big job.

**Z:** Yes, it is.

1. premises: 房屋及土地,经营场所

2. exploratory research: 探索性调研

## Dialogue 2

*Zhang Jian is discussing the market research project to be carried out by Li Yan's research team.*

**L:** Then what sort of research shall we carry out?

**Z:** Usually there are two main methods of research, questionnaires and interviews. As to questionnaires, there is a concept called validity[1] concerned, which means the ratio of the number of questionnaires you receive and the number of questionnaires you send out in your survey[2].

**L:** So the higher the ratio is, more valid our survey will be.

1. validity: 有效性

2. survey: 调查

**Z:** That's right.

**L:** How about the interview?

**Z:** It's a face-to-face survey. Research department is encouraged to hold focus groups of our major customers. Depth-interviews with leaders in foreign trade associations can be widely used. This would provide valid research results.

3. focus groups: 面对面,群体访谈

4. depth-interview: 面对面,一对一的访谈

**L:** Don't you think this would be more expensive? Why not use telephone interview?

**Z:** This might be another way out. But telephone interviews get lower response rate.

**L:** Oh, I see. In this case, we'd better use questionnaires to collect main information about our products, and use interviews to get some opinion to the market.

**Z:** You can try it!

# Practice

## Practice 1

In dialogue 1, Mr. Zhang is giving advice to Li Yan on what research information he needs to get and where to get the information. Please role-play dialogue 1 with the information you get in Warming Up exercises.

## Practice 2

With the help of your partner, please figure out the research methods mentioned in Dialogue 2. Make a dialogue with your partner on the advantages and disadvantages of each research method.

The following expressions may help you:

I feel that...

Don't you think...?

Why not...

## Practice 3

In Dialogue 2, Li Yan's team will use questionnaires to do market research. Suppose you are one of his team and will design a questionnaire to make a research on corn baskets. Explain the reason to support each question. The following is the sample of a questionnaire.

### Questionnaire on school website on campus

*Welcome to our market research.*

*Your three-minute participation is greatly appreciated.*

*All your answers will be kept secret. Only general results will be submitted for the final report.*

*Please tick the box which is most closely related to your reaction to the following statements or questions.*

1. How often do you browse websites?
   ___ daily          ___ weekly      ___ monthly      ___ hardly ever
2. In general, what do you think of the look of the site? (its colours, the font, graphics, etc.)
   ___ highly appealing    ___ good       ___ satisfactory    ___ disappointing
3. What feature of its look and feel do you like MOST? _____
   Why? _____
4. What feature of its look and feel do you like LEAST? _____
   Why? _____
5. Please comment on how easy it is to find your way around the site(e.g. from theme to theme and back to home again): _____
6. Is it always clear at all times where you are in the site?
   ___Yes        ___ No
   If No, please explain why you feel lost and perhaps suggest how we could avoid that: _____
   _____
7. Was the content easy to understand?
   ___Yes        ___ No
   If No, please explain why:_____
   _____
8. What forms of content would you like to see more of?
   ___text    ___images    ___video    ___ audio    ___downloadable documents
   ____others
9. Relative to what you are used to, describe the speed of the site generally.
   ___ fast    ___ reasonable    ___ slow    ___ frustratingly slow

## Practice 4

Please surf on the Internet and find more information such as purposes, approaches about market research. Make a presentation on the topic of market research to your class.

The following websites may help you:

www.rba.co.uk/sources/mr.htm

http://www.inc.com/guides/marketing/24018.html

# Learning More

### Market Research on the Internet

Some analysts predict that the Internet will soon be the primary market research tool. As the use of the Internet and online services becomes more of a habit than hype for more and more consumers, online research is becoming a quick, easy and inexpensive way to tap into their opinions. "Web users are a desirable group," observes Paul Jacobson, an executive of Greenfield Online—an online research company. "There are a great number of companies which want to reach that group because they are early adopters and leading-edge consumers."

Online users tend to be better educated, more affluent, and younger than average consumers. However, these are highly important consumers to companies offering products and services online. They are also some of the hardest to reach when conducting research. Online surveys and chat sessions often prove effective in getting elusive teens and single, affluent and well-educated audiences to participate.

**Questions for discussion:**

1. Do you agree with those analysts who predict that the Internet will soon be the primary market research tool? Please give reasons.
2. What are the characteristics of online users? Why do a great number of companies want to reach this group?

# Unit 2
## Market Analysis

# *Warming Up*

There are many useful expressions to describe market movements. Choose the right pattern in the given groups to describe the following charts and graph:

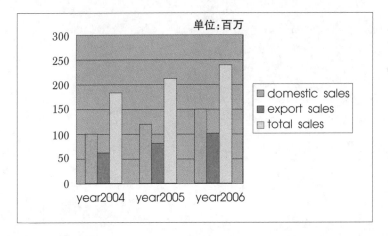

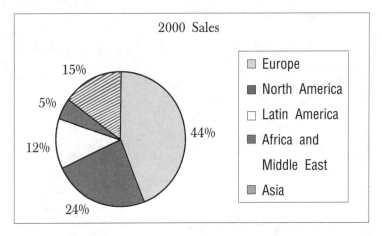

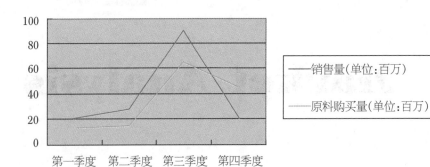

**Shares**

growing slowly/rapidly/quickly/swiftly/suddenly/steadily/gradually with...% in..., ...% in... and...% in ...

the total... market sums up to...% of...'s global sales

...occupied...% of...

...was a global company with...% sales outside Europe

...grow/rise/go up to/climb/boom//fall/decline/drop/go down/reduce to...% in Europe and ...% in North America

**Increase and decrease**

...sales rise up to $... in 19...

result in $...

It added $... to growth in 20...

raise... growth by $... to nearly $...

reach $... in 20... and target $... by 20...

...'s sales for the year move ahead by... to...

The growth... is $...

...sales in... market in 20... is only..., less than...% of market, despite a...% growth in 20...

**Highest and lowest**

highest point is...while lowest point is...

raise... for 20... to..., the highest in the recent... years

The remarkable... growth of...in the last 3... changes the landscape of...

reach its peak... and then drop sharply

climb steadily before falling slightly...

fall sharply before slowly recovering...

show a great improvement...

# *Situational Dialogues*

## Dialogue 1

*Li Yan is analyzing the market figures with Zhang Jian.*

**L:** After two months' research, through questionnaires and interviews, you know, we finally got all these figures.

**Z:** Good. Were there 5,560 sheets in this survey?

**L:** Oh, yes. Absolutely. They were carefully counted. But before we begin the discussion on the research results, Mr. Zhang, I think the vital thing I want to point out is the validity of that figure. In fact, there were 2,108 valid sheets, the rest of them are invalid because some of the questionnaires were answered improperly and some were even copies.

**Z:** Oh, what's the result?

**L:** As you can see from this graph, 80% of the receivers are interested in our corn baskets, and many of them are between 35—40.

**Z:** That means our customers will be the middle-aged people.

**L:** Yes. This pie graph shows the breakdown[1] of our customers. Middle-aged people accounts for 45%, our other two customer groups are 7—11 years old, at around 28 percent and old people, at 12 percent.

**Z:** How about the result of interview?

**L:** We have interviewed sales managers of 12 businesses, most of them show interest in our products.

**Z:** Excellent!

1. breakdown: 分类信息，分析

## Dialogue 2

*Li Yan is analyzing Boyi's major competitor, J&K Ltd., and predicting the European market with Zhang Jian.*

**L:** We conducted the interview in three main countries: Italy, France and Holand. 53% of French interviewees intend to know more about our products. Our interviewees also mentioned the main competitors in the market, they sell similar products to European customers.

**Z:** Who is our major competitor?

**L:** J&K Ltd. in Italy. We know that J&K is playing to win. And we know that right now they have the edge[1].

**Z:** So what are their advantages?

**L:** They have a larger market share; they have a cheaper product; and I think they have a larger advertising budget.

**Z:** That's critical. Who is their leading buyer?

**L:** Yada, it purchases around 45 percent of products from J& K.

**Z:** Do you expect Yada to purchase from us?

**L:** We hope so, if they increase their purchase and turn to us for some, we can share the market easily. As we predict, total market demand for this kind of products will increase over

1. the edge: 优势

the coming two years. Our goal is to have 30 percent of the market.

**Z:** There are two immediate things we can do: we can increase our advertising budget and make sure of our quality control.

# Practice

## Practice 1

**Use the expressions in Dialogue 1 and analyze the following charts.**

a. The pie chart below shows the ingredients used to make a sausage and mushroom pizza. The fraction of each ingredient by weight shown in the pie chart below is now given as a percentage.

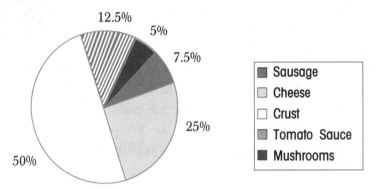

b. Bar graphs consist of an axis and a series of labeled horizontal or vertical bars that show different values for each bar. The numbers along the side of the bar graph are called the scale. The bar chart below shows the weight in kilograms of some fruits sold one day by a local market.

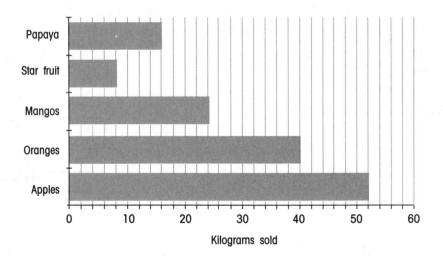

## Practice 2

According to Dialogue 2, J&K is the major competitor of Boyi Co.. Mr. Li Yan has worked out some strategies to counter competitors. Please discuss with your partner and try to find out as many strategies as you can to help Li Yan handle their competitors.

## Practice 3

In dialogue 1, Li Yan has described Boyi's current sales figures, market share, and customers. He is going to sell his products to European markets. Now he's making a report to the board of directors. Work in groups of 6, one acts as Li Yan, the others as members of board. Li Yan is trying to persuade them to put the new products on the European markets. You may cover the following points:

1. the demand for hand-made crafts in the European market
2. the Chinese export volume on hand-made crafts
3. the major competitors against Boyi in the European market
4. Boyi's competitive advantage in the European market

## Practice 4

Market analysis includes internal analysis and external analysis. Commonly, internal analysis refers to the analysis within the company like SWOT analysis, which refers to Strength, Weakness, Opportunities and Threats. Please discuss with your partner about Boyi's internal analysis.

Strength:
Weakness:
Opportunities:
Threats:

# Learning More

## Market Analysis in Practice

The goal of a market analysis is to determine the attractiveness of a market and to understand its evolving opportunities and threats as they relate to the strengths and weaknesses of the firm. Let's have a look at the following dimensions of a market analysis:

- ☆ Market size (current and future)
- ☆ Market growth rate
- ☆ Key success factors

### Market Size

The size of the market can be evaluated based on present sales and on potential sales if the use of the product were expanded.

### Market Trends

Changes in the market are important because they often are the source of new opportunities and threats. The relevant trends are industry-dependent, but some examples include changes in price sensitivity, demand for variety, and level of emphasis on service and support. Regional trends also may be relevant.

### Key Success Factors

The key success factors are those elements that are necessary in order for the firm to achieve its marketing objectives. A few examples of such factors include:

- ☆ Access to essential and unique resources
- ☆ Ability to achieve economies of scale
- ☆ Access to distribution channels
- ☆ Technological progress

**Questions for discussion:**

1. What is the goal of a market analysis?
2. What key factors are necessary for the success?

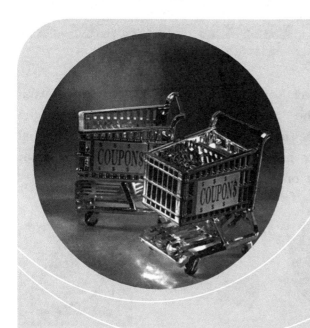

# Unit 3

# Sales Promotion

# Warming Up

1. So far as you know from all sources of media in your life, what promotional activities do the manufactuers hold for the following products? Please list for the following pictures as many promotional activities as you can. Compare notes with your partner and discuss what activity is the most impressive one.

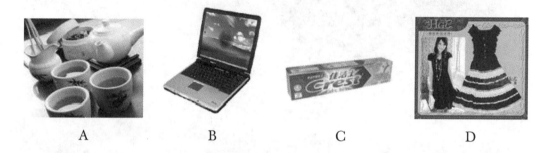

| A | B | C | D |

2. A good sales promoter should be familiar with customers' psychology and adopt different promotional techniques to different people. Discuss with your partner and highlight the technique you will use when you are promoting the same product to different kinds of people.

   (a) a housewife

   (b) a foreigner

   (c) a young couple

# Situational Dialogues

## Dialogue 1

*After market investigation, Li Yan decided to put corn baskets on European Markets. Now, he is talking with Mr. zhang about sales promotion.*

**L:** As we don't understand much about the EU market, my biggest concern is how sales promotional activities can function well with the expanding of the market. We believe your expert opinion will help us a lot. Could you give us some tips?

**Z:** As we know, there are many ways to push sales, for example,

TV ads, network, publicity[1], exhibition, agency, etc. These strategies can be adapted to the EU market. By comparison, TV ads are the most effective way.

**L:** For sure, but TV ads will cost a lot of money, I suppose. And at the preliminary stage, TV ads may not exert its positive impact on[2] those potential customers in the European market. What we need to do at the moment is just to inform.

**Z:** So you should work out a careful plan before guiding your campaign to success. Taking a financial budget into account, the first thing is decide what media you should use and place an advertisement on it. Yet, this kind of medium should be cost-effective[3] and can exert the biggest influence on foreign customers.

**L:** I see. Our team will work out the overall plan in a few days.

1. publicity: (杂志、报纸或电视的)关注，报道，宣传

2. exert its positive impact on...: 施加积极的影响……

3. cost-effective: 有成本效益的，值得花费的，合算的

## Dialogue 2

*Several days later, Mr. Li Yan is having a discussion with his manager on a planned sales promotion scheme[1].*

**L:** Our team has drafted a sales promotion scheme after consulting Sales Promotion Services Inc. The overall plan will be implemented by using a combination of media, and meanwhile, we'll find some influential agents in this sector to improve business.

**M:** Could you be more specific?

**L:** At the introduction stage, to help people know more about our products, we will seek an influential expert publisher in the overseas market. We'll take the front page to advertise our products. Meanwhile, we'll give access[2] to the corn baskets together with other Boyi products on Boyi web pages. To gain more recognition, we'll participate in some exhibitions. If possible, we'll also find some agents to cover the European areas.

**M:** It sounds good. What about the operational cost for the preliminary stage? Does it meet your financial budget?

**L:** After calculation, all costs for the preliminary stage will not exceed RMB¥500,000.

**M:** All right.

1. sales promotion scheme: 促销计划

2. access: 享用机会，享用权；通道，入口

# Practice

Practice 1

**Task 1:** According to Dialogue 1 and 2, Mr. Li Yan has mentioned some promotional methods. Work with your partner to pick them out and list more.

**Task 2:** Jenny is working as a sales representative in G&M Company. Now she is planning to push sales of G&M mobile phones by emphasizing their economy, energy conservation, easy operation and freedom from multifunction. Please help Jenny pick out the appropriate promotional method(s) from your lists and explain your reason.

Practice 2

Advertising is considered as one of the most effective promotion activities. It may help people make a purchase decision when they are at a loss to face so many choices.

Please discuss the following questions with your partner:

What are TV commercials that appeal to you most? Why do you like them?

Which ones have made you impulsive in buying?

Are there any commercials you don't like? How would you improve them?

Practice 3

Your group is supposed to role play an advertisement of your own. Make it funny, creative and impressive. Let other groups tell what product you are advertising.

E. Modern is a newly opened restaurant on the 8th floor of a 10-floor shopping mall on the outskirts of Shanghai. They specialize in western style food with special Chinese-western mixed style of lunch package. To promote sales, they have advertised their restaurant in a monthly fashion magazine and distributed coupons to any visiting customer, but coupons received can't be used on the same consuming day. In addition, everyday the first 10 customers can have one drink free. Ten weeks since opening, the restaurant has enjoyed bleak business.

Please work in groups and try to figure out the problem in sales promotion of the restaurant and then make an oral report to the whole class on how to solve these problems.

# Learning More

### Promotional Tools

Promotion is the most important in a product's introduction and maturity stages. The major promotional tools are advertising, personal selling, sales promotion and publicity. In introduction, the market is unaware of the product and therefore uninterested, and promotion must overcome ignorance and generate interest. In the maturity stage, competition is stiff and the promotion must show how a product is different or unique. In addition, promotional mix policies are affected by promotional program objectives implementing strategies evaluation of program effectiveness and the promotional budget.

All in all, promotional tools should be used to communicate a message to a person or appropriate target market in order to elicit a favorable response—such as purchasing or attitude change. Although there is no universally acceptable correct mix for all organizations, one should always bear the following in mind: Who is the target market? What is the message that I want to convey? And how can I best communicate that sort of message to that target market?

**Questions for discussion:**

According to the passage, promotional activities can be divided into two stages. Can you tell the differences between strategies used in each stage? What are the differences? Share your answers with your group members.

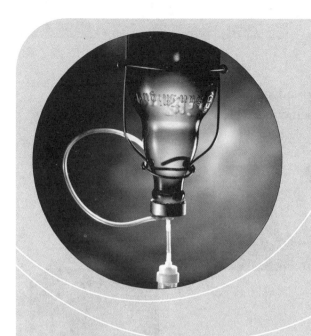

# Unit 4

## Advertising

# Warming Up

1.  What do the following posters advertise?
2.  Among the following advertisements, which impressed you most? Why?

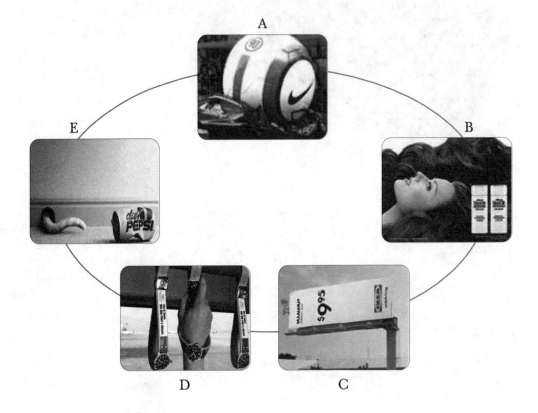

A

E

B

D

C

# Situational Dialogues

### Dialogue 1

*Li Yan is talking with Zhang Jian about the advertising campaign for the company's new product— corn baskets.*

**L:** So, what's the status of our advertising campaign?
**Z:** As I mentioned before, it'll be a campaign starting next month. We've selected France as our priority, and we'll use a variety of media for full coverage. First, we will have a 30-second spot

on television once a day for 3 weeks. At the same time, we'll do 15-second radio commercials 3 times a day. These television and radio programs are open to the main cities in France. Then, we'll have some outdoor ads using billboards near main entrances to big cities. Finally, we will design new website and participate a trade fair to promote our products.

**L:** What style will the ads use?

**Z:** We're focusing on slice of life[1], showing how you can ornament[2] your room with some corn products. These adverts are trying to attract people's attention by using models and actresses; then shift the people's focus to having a nice corn product.

**L:** Sounds like an ideal approach. Will we have a new slogan[3]?

**Z:** Definitely. The advertising agency's working on that right now. They'll have some proposals ready by the end of the week.

**L:** Sounds like we'll have a winner on our hands!

1. slice of life: 现实生活的描写, 日常生活的写照
2. ornament: 装饰,点缀,美化
3. slogan: 广告语; 标语

## Dialogue 2

*Li Yan is discussing about a TV commercial with Zhang Jian.*

**L:** What is the main goal we want to achieve with the advertisement?

**Z:** We would like to establish our product in the European market and increase customer awareness.

**L:** Of the four major types of mass media, TV is best at communicating images and symbols because they can demonstrate our product usage and arose consumer reactions.

**Z:** Yes, in fact, they have enormous reach[1]—almost all European households have a TV set, so we're looking for someone to design and make a TV commercial for our new products.

**L:** What kind of audience would we like to target?

**Z:** Now we want to aim at multiple targets of 35—40 year olds and 7—11 year olds. They should be wealthy, successful or playful.

**L:** I see. As the products target the high-end market, consumers are those who care more about the styles and quality of the

1. enormous reach: 极大的促及面

products instead of price. In other words, they are not price sensitive. So what kind of message do you want to convey to our potential consumers?

**Z:** We expect them to recognize that we're the best corn products manufacturer in China. Our products are the symbol of their social status and high quality life.

**L:** OK. I will make an appointment with ABC Advertising Agency to talk about our TV commercial.

# Practice

## Practice 1

Work in pairs. One student, as the owner of an ice-cream manufacturing company, is talking with the other student, the marketing manager, about the advertising campaign for the company's new ice-cream sandwich. Try to rehearse Dialogue 1, the following sentence patterns may be also helpful.

1. We are going to start the campaign by putting full page ads in all the major newspapers over a period of a month.
2. They'll be in weekly, probably on every Monday, and after that we are planning to focus on TV and radio.
3. What are the advertising rates in the Sunday edition of... Newspaper?
4. It will be best to insert advertisements in the leading newspapers of our most important cities.
5. The designer should be familiar with the character of our products.

## Practice 2

Try to rehearse Dialogue 2 and work in pairs. One is the marketing director from Golden Sun Hotel, and the other is the accounting director of an advertising agency named New Creation. The hotel has decided to design and make a TV commercial to promote the hotel. They are talking about the aim of the commercial, the target market of the hotel and budget set by the hotel.

### Information Sheet of the Hotel

The hotel has 100 rooms and is 5 years old. It has a very nice restaurant with a unique menu featuring a weekly pig roast and a Sunday morning brunch. There is an excellent outdoor patio bar with special island drinks. Native groups furnish evening music for listening and dancing. It is located on an outer island, far away from the noise. The only way to get to the island is by boat or to fly from Miami. Round trip fare by boat is $65 and by plane $100.

## Practice 3

Work in groups. One member of the group is the chairperson. Each group is a team in the Marketing Department. Hold a meeting to discuss what you should do to advertise your product: a new ice cream.

### SPECIFIC GUIDELINES

1. Each group will develop an advertising campaign over a one-month period of time while following a specified budget.
2. Establish goals for the campaign.
3. Select the media to be used and explain why.

    NOTE: You must use at least three of the media listed below in your campaign.

| | |
|---|---|
| TV | Direct Mail |
| Radio | Outdoor |
| Newspaper | Magazine |

## Practice 4

**Presentation: Bad Advertisements Vs. Good Advertisements**

Find a total of ten ads from newspaper, magazines, TV, radio and so on. Five of these ads, in your mind, are good advertisements while the other five belong to the category of bad advertisements. Discuss with your classmates what makes good advertisements?

# Learning More

## Successful Advertising Campaign

There are five main stages in a well-managed advertising campaign:

**Stage 1: Set Advertising Objectives**

An advertising objective is a specific communication task to be achieved with a specific target audience during a specific period of time.

**Stage 2: Set the Advertising Budget**

Setting the advertising budget is not easy—how can a business predict the right amount to spend. Which parts of the advertising campaign will work best and which will have relatively little effect? Often businesses use "rules-of-thumb" (e.g. advertising/sales ratio) as a guide to set the budget.

**Stage 3: Determine the key Advertising Message**

The advertising message must be carefully targeted to impact the target customer audience. A successful advertising message should have the following characteristics:

(a) Meaningful

(b) Distinctive

(c) Believable

**Stage 4: Decide which Advertising Media to Use**

There are a variety of advertising media from which to choose. A campaign may use one or more of the media alternatives. The key factors in choosing the right media include:

(a) Reach

(b) Frequency

(c) Media Impact

**Stage 5: Evaluate the results of the Advertising Campaign**

The evaluation of an advertising campaign should focus on two key areas:

(1) The Communication Effects is the intended message being communicated effectively and to the intended audience.

(2) The Sales Effects the campaign has generated the intended sales growth.

**Questions for discussion:**

1. What are the main stages in a well-managed advertising campaign?

2. What are the key areas when we evaluate the advertising campaign?

# Unit 5

# Trade Fair

# Warming Up

1. Have you ever been to an exhibition before?
2. Please talk with your partner and describe a common exhibition show. The following list of things may help you.

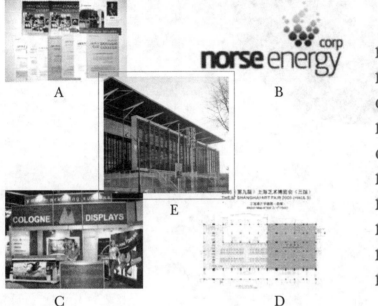

A

B

C

E

D

Exhibition hall

Exhibition booth

Company logo

Brochures

Catalogues

Flyers

Free sample

Free gifts

Personal interviews

Informal negotiations

# Situational Dialogues

## Dialogue 1

Li Yan has received an invitation to China Import and Export Fair in Guangzhou. Now he is talking with Zhang Jian about the exhibition.

**L:** Mr. Zhang, we've just received an invitation to China Import and Export Fair in Guangzhou with the participation fee of RMB20,000. Do you think we could accept the invitation?

**Z:** To be frank, the fee is quite reasonable for such an exposure. The possibility of participation mainly depends on its effectiveness[1].

**L:** Effectiveness? I'd like to have your idea on effectiveness.

**Z:** Yes, an effective participation can bring about rewarding results,

1. effectiveness:
产生预想效果

and help meet the company objectives. Guangzhou Fair has become an international fair, well-known to many businesses abroad.

**L:** So, the trade fair could help improve our company image and crack open the overseas market for our corn baskets series.

**Z:** That's right.

**L:** Then we can go ahead.

**Z:** But before the fair, you have to book booth, send samples, decorate the booth and have enough staff equipped for the fair.

**L:** Can you be more specific?

**Z:** Well, generally speaking, careful planning seems to be particularly important. The location of the booth shall suit your need and be easy for visitors to access. The booth shall help attract the people in, and samples on display shall help establish our image.

**L:** I see.

## Dialogue 2

*Several days later, Li Yan and Mr. Zhang arrived at the exhibition hall to check the booth decoration.*

**Z:** Take a look! We've taken No. 10 booth[1], quite close to the entrance.

**L:** Yes, we choose the right location for our goods.

**Z:** Ah, I like the background color! The golden logo in the middle is set against the green background. Exquisite design!

**L:** Yeah, the design style fits in well with the baskets. I believe our products will be in the spotlight[2] at the exhibition.

**Z:** Definitely.

**L:** At the moment, we still have a lot to do. We need to confirm the attendance of some invitees, and we have to get more catalogues printed.

**Z:** Just a reminder. Not all for catalogues. Catalogues can be distributed to those potential customers. Try to prepare some flyers[3].

**L:** Flyers?

**Z:** Yes. Flyers for those visitors who just come and have a look. It'll save you costs.

**L:** That's a good idea.

1. booth: 展位, 摊位

2. In the spotlight: 为公众所瞩目

3. flyer: 小传单, 小广告

# *Practice*

## Practice 1

As from Dialogue 1, upon receipt of an invitation to a trade fair, you will decide if you attend and the important things you shall clear up before the fair. Exchange ideas with your partner on the preparation for exhibition.

## Practice 2

Floral Company is a food company. They are seeking an exhibition expert to design their booth for East China Food Exhibition, which will last for 3 days. You are required to work out the lay-out of the booth as follows:

Floral Logo

platform installation for the product demonstration

products display (cola, beer, drinks, etc.)

color of the whole booth

Please work in groups and make a draft design of the booth. Then explain why you design your booth that way. The picture on the right may give you some idea.

## Practice 3

G&M will participate in East China Electronics Exhibition. Do you have any idea about what a company does in advance before an exhibition? According to the clues below, please help to make an agenda by arranging events in priority for G&M for the upcoming three-day exhibition from 20 Sept. to 22 Sept. Then explain why you make such arrangements.

Booth and platform set-up

Product A (G&M mobile phone) Demonstration

Product B (G&M electronic dictionary) Demonstration

Question & Answer Session

Catalogue Distribution

Removal of platform and booth

**G&M's Exhibition Plan for**

**East China Electronics Exhibition**

**20–22 September**

**Date          Event          People in charge**

## Practice 4

Discuss with your partner on how to measure the effectiveness of participation in trade fair. Then suppose you have the final say in the following case, will you decide to go or not? Why or why not? Divide your class into two groups and argue with each other.

At a monthly sales meeting, Irene, Production Manager of a textile company suggested that they should go to the International Textile Exposition to be held in Tokyo because the exposition would be an ideal place to present their new products. Only two regional sales managers agreed to the idea and the other four thought that the exposition was not worthwhile attending because the estimated cost of RMB¥200, 000 meant a large sum for a medium-sized enterprise.

# *Learning More*

### Why Visit an Exhibition

There are many ways of collecting products and supplier information, but only exhibitions allow you to put suppliers' claims comprehensively to the test by examining the products yourself, questioning their creators, comparing and contrasting their performance specifically. Visitors attend exhibitions to

**See what's new**

Exhibitions are a recognized launch pad for new products and an extremely efficient way to keep up to date with the latest innovations.

**Evaluate products and suppliers**

You can compile a wide range of competitive information on products and suppliers in a concentrated period of time.

**Keep informed of industry and market developments**

Exhibitions are a rich source of new ideas and applications and they play an important role in strategic planning and business generation.

**Network/Develop business contacts**

Exhibitions are a focal point for industry, attracting a broad cross-section of representatives, from buyers and sellers to trade associations and the media.

**Other common reasons for attending exhibitions include:**

to consolidate business relationships

to solve specific problems

to find new markets

to appoint agents/seek principals

to discuss specific terms/conditions/pricing

to obtain technical knowledge

to discuss business needs in a neutral environment

**Questions for discussion:**

1. What are the possible reasons for visiting an exhibition?
2. Do you think that exhibitions may help develop business contacts? Why or why not?

# Unit 6

## Brand Power

# Warming Up

**Read the following introduction to the product features and match these products with their features.**

"I'm Bryan from G&M Trading Company. We appreciate your interest in our electric products. I'm pleased to give you a brief introduction of the products included in our catalogue.

Our electric fans are of a special design;

We have a good variety of radios;

We guarantee that the watches we produce are resistant to water;

Our rice cookers save you money;

Our video players are well-known throughout the world;

Our cameras are popular among young people;

Our telephones can be used for a long time , simple-looking though;

We are launching a new style of video camera as you can see from the picture in our catalogue."

| Features | Products |
| --- | --- |
| particular | rice cooker |
| fashionable | electric fan |
| durable | cameras |
| famous brand | video player |
| latest model | telephone |
| reasonable price | radios |
| waterproof | video camera |
| wide selection | watch |

# Situational Dialogues

## Dialogue 1

*Li Yan meets Susan, a representative from Masaic International Corporation from France at the exhibition.*

**L:** Good morning, Ma'am. What can I do for you?

**S:** Ah, I'm a representative from Mosaic International Corporation from France. My name is Susan.

**L:** Glad to see you Susan. I'm Li Yan from Boyi Arts Trading Company.

**S:** Nice to meet you too, Mr. Li. I'm interested in your basket products. They look nice and very stylish[1]!

1. stylish: 时髦的

**L:** I appreciate your interest. I have some catalogues for you.

**S:** Thank you. Do these cover all of your products?

**L:** Yes, everything we export is included, and we highly recommend to you our newly developed ones—"corn baskets."

**S:** Can you tell me more about it?

**L:** Here is a sample for you. Well, we are testing the market now.

**S:** How soon is this product going to be on the market?

**L:** Later next month, but obviously we are starting the publicity campaign[2] before then.

2. publicity campaign: 宣传运动

**S:** I'm glad to hear that.

**L:** This is our website and my business card as well. If anything I can help, don't hesitate to contact me.

**S:** Okay, thank you Mr. Li. This is my card.

**L:** Well. Hope to see you again soon.

## Dialogue 2

*Two days later, Li Yan is busy at the trade fair. Susan comes to see him again.*

**L:** Hello, Susan. Nice to see you again. Anything I can do for you?

**S:** Yes. Last night I browsed some of your web pages, and got to know your branded products gained popularity in Guangzhou for their good design and fine quality.

**L:** Thank you for your attention. All of our products including the corn baskets are hand-woven with natural materials.

**S:** That sounds good. But the materials of the corn baskets seem to be a bit different from the others'.

**L:** A shrewd eyesight! For corn baskets, we use the corns coated with a kind of untoxic substance. In the weaving process, technicians mix the natural corns with silver strings and leather strips to hand weave them.

**S:** Well, your fine craftsmanship makes the products unique.

**L:** Yeah. The blended use of the material, you know, improves its durability[1] and makes it waterproof[2]. Even in the humid weather, it may not go deformed or eroded. For this, our corn baskets have got certified by ISO9002.

**S:** That's amazing.

1. durability: 耐用, 持久
2. waterproof: 防水的

# *Practice*

### Practice 1

According to Dialogue 1&2, please have a discussion with your partner on the following questions:

1. What are the product features of the corn baskets?
2. What make the corn baskets different from the others of its kind?
3. Of all these features from Question 2, which can appeal to the potential buyers most? And Why?

### Practice 2

Select one of the products in the following and describe one to your partner without telling him the name of commodity. Your partner will try to guess what it is.

| | | | |
|---|---|---|---|
| MP4 | digital camera | electric motor | refrigerator | rechargeable battery |
| air conditioner | tea-pot | mobile phone | glasses | healthy food |

### Practice 3

Examine the following list of product features. Suppose you are a member from a foreign purchasing team. You are having a meeting discussing which of the following features you will give top consideration to when placing an order for video cameras. Select four of them and give your reasons justifying your choice and present it to the whole class.

| | | |
|---|---|---|
| particular | fashionable | big storage |
| latest model | famous brand | clear picture |
| durable | reasonable price | multi-functional |
| waterproof | smooth operation | professional |

## Practice 4

Discuss with your partner the last purchase you made. Tell each other why you bought it instead of another substitute. For example, your last purchase was a watch made in Switzerland. Tell your partner why you did not buy a watch made in China which is of the same price. Do you think a watch made in Switzerland and a watch made in China are the same? If not, what makes them different?

# Learning More

### Product Presentation Strategies

Why do people prefer certain styles, types or brands of products to others? Buyers' choices may be affected by a brand image or the package, warranty, color, design or another feature of the product. Among them brand and package are the most common two.

**Branding**

Perhaps the most distinctive skill of professional marketers is their ability to create, maintain, protect and enhance the brands of their products and services. Branding helps buyers in many ways. Brand names help consumers identify products that might benefit them. Brands also tell the buyers something about product quality. Buyers who always buy the same brand know that they will get the same feature, benefits and quality each time they buy. Branding also gives the seller several advantages. The seller's brand name and trademark provide legal protection for unique product features that otherwise might be copied by competitors. Branding also helps the seller to segment the market.

**Packaging**

Packaging involves designing and producing the container or wrapper for a product. Traditionally, the primary function of a package was to contain and protect the product. In recent times, however, numerous factors have made packaging an important marketing tool. Increased competition and clutter on retail store shelves means that packages must now perform many sales tasks from attracting attention, to describing the product, to making the sale. In this highly competitive environment, the package may be the seller's last chance to influence buyers. It becomes a "five-second commercial".

**Questions for discussion:**
1. Why do business people brand their products?
2. What are the functions of packaging?

# Unit 7

## Corporation Introduction

# Warming Up

1. Try to talk about the type of company you would most like to work for after graduation. The following lists may help you.

| Nature | Size | Others |
|---|---|---|
| Family-owned | small | standardization |
| State-operated | medium-sized | customization |
| Private-owned | multinational | work environment |
| | trans-national | location |
| | | pay, promotion |
| | | job security |

A

B

C

2. Brainstorm on the aspects from which we may introduce a company?

# Situational Dialogues

## Dialogue 1

As Susan is very interested in the exhibits of Boyi Arts Trading Company, she is now talking to Li Yan for more information about his company at the Fair.

**S:** I'm fascinated by your splendid exhibits. Your company must have a long history in this line.

**L:** Yes, indeed. Our company has specialized in making arts and crafts of the botanical materials for nearly 30 years and it started with a small factory in the early 1970s.

**S:** A small factory? But from your bulletin board, I can see your company has really developed very quickly.

**L:** You bet. We have expanded our factory with more than 200 experienced workers, and established over 30 sales outlets[1] across the country and a headquarter dealing with the

1. outlet: 经销点, 商店

domestic and overseas orders.

**S:** So you also export your products to Europe?

**L:** Not yet. We have made market research in Europe and find a potential market there. We are endeavoring[2] to expand our market share in some European countries.

**S:** That indicates a possibility for us to establish a long business relationship. I think these products will be loved by French people.

**L:** I'm glad to hear that. We hope you can join hands with us.

**S:** Would you mind giving me more detailed information about your company?

**L:** No problem.

## Dialogue 2

*Li Yan handed a brochure about his company's profiles to Susan and continued the talk.*

**L:** Here is our company's brochure. You may read it and get some ideas.

**S:** Thank you. Is this your company? (*Pointing to a picture of a building in the brochure.*)

**L:** Yes, it is our headquarter.

**S:** It enjoys such a beautiful sea view.

**L:** Yes. It is located to the southeast of Guangzhou and thus right on the coast.

**S:** So you are easily accessible[1] by road and ship.

**L:** Also by rail and air as Guangzhou is a very large transportation hub[2] in the south.

**S:** Well, could you tell me the daily output of your factory?

**L:** It depends. Take corn baskets for example, we have a daily capacity of 500 baskets.

**S:** Very impressive. Could I know your trade principle?

**L:** We do our business on the basis of equality and mutual benefit. One can always expect a fair deal when trading with us.

**S:** We shall be happy to do business with you on these principles.

**L:** In recent years, we have won recognition in this business and enjoy a reputation for high quality.

**S:** We highly appreciate it.

**L:** We often stick to our belief: Customer first, quality superior.

**S:** I see. It is really worthwhile to establish a business partnership with you. That's because of both your credibility and your fantastic products.

# Practice

## Practice 1

Work in pairs, student A plays the role of Susan and student B acts as Li Yan, re-introduce the Boyi company with the expressions in Warming Up and information in dialogues. The following sentence patterns may be also helpful.

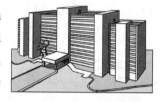

How old is your company?

How is your business going?

What do you specialize in?

Can I have a brochure of your company?

Where is your company located?

What is the total annual output of the factory?

Do you sell your products domestically or internationally?

Our company is a state-owned unit founded .../Our development can trace back to...

We mainly deal with.../manufacture...

It is situated..., just 30 minutes drive from airport./easily accessible by the road.

Our products are the best sellers both at home and abroad.

We persist in the principle of .../adopted a policy of...

## Practice 2

**Pair work**

Make an introduction of the following company to your partner with the help of the listed fact and then let your partner to summarize what you have introduced.

| | |
|---|---|
| **Name:** | Shanghai Power Electric CO LTD |
| **Nature:** | A High-Tech joint venture(SIA Group and Shanghai Hujiang Electric Science & Technology Ltd) |
| **Location:** | Pudong New Area, about 15 minutes' drive from Pudong Airport. |
| **Scale:** | Over 20 Senior Engineers and over 300 Junior Engineers. |
| **Scope:** | Electric power and electronic products. |
| **Feature:** | 36 years R&D and manufacturing experience in inverter products. |
| **Strength:** | An effective management system and a high effitient quality control system according to ISO9000 |
| **Guidance:** | "Surviving based on the quality of products; Developing based on R&D and exploiting market by maintaining high service level". |
| **Commitment:** | Perfect technical support and after-sales services |

## Practice 3

**Role-play**

1. **Student A acts as the Marketing Manager of China Pacific Insurance Company Ltd. and student B is a very important client, who wants to get some detailed information about the company. Therefore, students A is having a conversation with student B to provide him with the information listed in the following profiles.**

### China Pacific Insurance Company Ltd.

China Pacific Insurance Company Ltd. is a joint stock limited company. It is the second largest nationwide insurance company in China, the registered capital of which is one billion Yuan (RMB). Its head office is situated in Shanghai.

China Pacific Insurance Company has more than 50 subsidiaries all over the country. The head office has appointed more than one hundred agents at various important ports and cities in over sixty countries and districts throughout the world to conduct survey on cargoes, settle claims and effect recoveries on its behalf. And now it has offices in New York, London and Hong Kong.

China Pacific Insurance Company will persist in its principle: Serve its Chinese and foreign clients with first-rate service quality, first-rate work efficiency and first-rate company reputation.

The scope of business:

(1) To underwrite different sorts of insurance, either in RMB or foreign currency.

(2) To transact reinsurance business at home and abroad and statutory insurance.

(3) To invest in securities and deal with other financial transactions.

(4) To establish agency relationship with Chinese and foreign insurance institutions and participate in international insurance activities.

No.3 Nanhai Road, Qingdao, China Tel: 2863010 Fax: 2865680

**2. Student A acts as a sales manager from Shanghai Textile Corporation, and Student B acts as Mr. Johnson, a businessman from Russia who is ready to develop a business partnership with Student A's Corporation. Therefore, Student A is introducing his company in great details to student B to arouse his interest.**

Some basic facts about this company:

(1) specializing in the bed linen covering bed sheets, pillow cases, bed spread

(2) a long history

(3) computerized production lines

(4) easily accessible

(5) Motto: to satisfy every customer's special needs

## Practice 4

### Presentation

You are required to use the library and Internet resources to find out the information of your favorite company. Make a presentation to introduce this company to your classmates including the following basic facts:

History and development

Location and accessibility

Ownership and scope of business

Size and capability

Strength & special features

Management idea or service philosophy

# Learning More

### Prospectus (Finance)

A prospectus is a legal document that institutions and businesses use to describe what they have to offer for participants and buyers. A prospectus is commonly used to detail mutual funds, stocks, and other investments. The documents go into detail about a business, providing a history of the company, lists of officers who operate such a business, any litigation that is taking place, financial data, and a list of operations. These documents, when used by businesses, are usually given out to potential investors as part of the Initial Public Offering (IPO). Although usually very detailed, the public prospectuses are usually very condensed compared to the registration statements filed with the US Securities and Exchange Commission (SEC).

In the United States, prospectuses are used by countless industries outside of the stock investment world as well. Having been a standard in the film business since the early years of the motion picture industry, a prospectus is regarded by most producers as the practical catalyst for financing a project.

Prospectuses are generally prepared by an Issue Manager. The Issue Manager prepares the prospectus with the help of information supplied by the issuer (the Company). The Issue Manager may also take part in discussions with the Chairman, Managing Director and other executives of the company in preparing the prospectus.

**Questions for discussion:**

1. List some basic facts about a financial prospectus, like purpose, content, etc.
2. How is a general introduction of a company different from the prospectus in terms of finance?

# Unit 8

## Invitation

# Warming Up

1. What should you do if someone only invites you, but doesn't say what the invitation is for?
2. Do you know how to refuse an invitation?

# Situational Dialogues

## Dialogue 1

*Susan finished talking with Li Yan about their business.*

**S:** Well, it's been good to meet you, Mr. Li, and very interesting to hear about your business.

**L:** Look, we are having a small dinner for some of our clients and friends after this. Why don't you join us?

**S:** That's very kind of you. I'll just check with my associate whether she has other arrangements.

**L:** Your associate is most welcome to join us too.

**S:** Thank you. Excuse me, Celia, Mr. Li has very kindly invited us to a dinner.

**L:** Yes, would you like to join us?

**C:** Unfortunately I have another engagement, but thank you for the invitation.

**L:** Well, perhaps you could join us after that for a drink?

**C:** Sounds great. I'd be happy to. Where shall we meet?

**L:** How about the lounge bar here. At about ten?

**C:** I'll see you then.

**L:** Well, shall we make a move?

**S:** Okay.

*During the dinner, Li Yan invited Susan to visit his factory in China.*

**L:** If you'd like, we'd be delighted to see you at our workshop.

**S:** It's very kind of you. My associate and I would be interested in visiting your factory.

**L:** Let us know when you are free. We'll arrange the tour for you.

**S:** Thanks. There's nothing like seeing things with one's own eyes.

**L:** That's for sure. You will know our products better after the visit.

**S:** Yes.

**L:** How long will you be in China? When is OK with you?

**S:** We'll be here for another three weeks, for other business of course. We want to visit next week, about November 1st.

**L:** I'm glad to hear that, but we'll have a business tour of seven days from November 1st to 7th. Could you change the time?

**S:** That is all right. Business always comes first. En November 8th?

**L:** OK, I am really sorry for the delay. Could you give me your email address? I'll arrange your tour and email the schedule to you.

**S:** Thanks a lot. My email address is *susan@masaic.com*

**L:** I've got it. I am looking forward to seeing you.

# *Practice*

Try to rehearse Dialogue 1&2 with the substitution of the following sentence patterns.

**Offer an invitation**

I would like to invite you to a dinner...

Would you like to...?

**Accept an invitation**

Thanks, I'd love to very much.

That sounds like a good idea.

**Refuse an invitation**

It's very kind of you to invite me, but I'm expecting some visitors this evening.

If you don't mind, I'd rather not. I'm tied up this week.

Unfortunately I have another engagement.

## Practice 2

Work in pairs.  One of you is the Marketing Director of a wine manufacturer. The other is the British Sales Manager.  Role play a telephone call about an invitation to a plant of clothing.

**SPECIFIC GUIDELINES**

1. A gives B an invitation.
2. B refuses the invitation with a reason.
3. A suggests another time.
4. B expresses thanks.

**Or**

1. A gives B an invitation.
2. B accept the invitation.
3. A suggests the specific time to meet.
4. B agrees and expresses thanks.

## Practice 3

Role play this situation. One is a boss of a patch work quilt company, and the other is a potential investor.  The boss is at a conference.  He recognizes a venture investor he met at a conference two years ago.  The boss tries to invite the potential investor to visit his company.

**Work in groups.**

Imagine that you work in an office. The company wants to organize a party for the important client.

Think about your answers to the questions below.

☆ What kind of party would the client like: a meal in a restaurant, a disco, a drink party? Where would the client like the party to be?

☆ What day of the week would the client prefer for the party? What time should it start and finish?

☆ Who should be invited to the party: only the important client, a client and his partners, a client and his wife?

Now work with your group. The boss has called a meeting to discuss the party. Share your opinions and decide what sort of party you are going to have.

# Learning More

### Differences in Declining an Invitation

Most people in the West don't like to give detailed explanations why they're declining an invitation. Their explanations are usually short and simple, such as "I'm sorry, I can't get away "or "I'm tied up the whole week" or "I'm already busy that night."

While in China, people will give a more detailed explanation to make sure that the person doing the inviting will understand that there is something important that must be done, or a prior engagement has already been made.

The purpose is "to give the other person face", to reassure him or her of the speaker's esteem for the inviter. Thus, the Chinese detailed explanation sounds unnecessary to the Westerner, and the Westerner's short, undetailed explanation sounds impolite to the Chinese, since both are unaware of each other's customs.

What's more, sometimes to be polite, the Chinese will even pretend to want to come and promise to try to come by saying "我尽量来"(I'll try my best to come). However, a misunderstanding will occur in the intercultural communication. To a Chinese, the saying "try my best" means the person may or may not come, but will sincerely try, but to the Westerner it doesn't sound sincere, but hypocritical.

http://beta.zjtvu.edu.cn/bmwy/wyx/CCC/unit4/index.htm

**Questions for discussion:**

What are the cultural differences in declining invitation?

# Unit 9

## Visiting a Plant

# Warming Up

Some visitors are coming to your factory. Look at the following organization chart and think which areas you would show them. Arrange a day's activity for them. The following words may be useful in your activity.

Plant / Supply area / Assembly area / Dispatch area / Raw materials conveyor

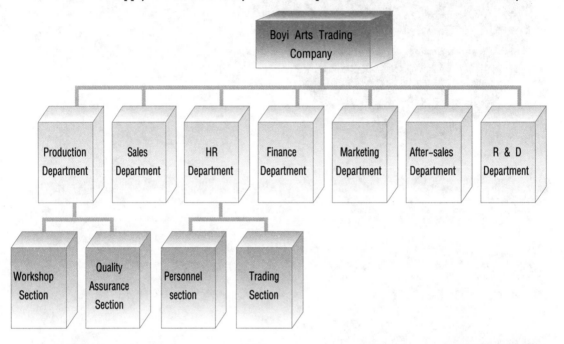

# Situational Dialogues

## Dialogue 1

*Susan arrives at Boyi, and Li Yan is showing her around.*

**L:** Hello, Susan. Nice to meet you... and welcome to Boyi.

**S:** Hello. Nice to meet you too.

**L:** Let me tell you about factory while I show you around, OK?

**S:** Good idea.

**L:** That is our office block. We have all the administrative departments there. Down there is the research and development section.

**S:** How much do you spend on development every year?

**L:** About 5—6% of the gross sales.

**S:** What's that building opposite us?

**L:** That's the warehouse. We keep a stock of the faster moving items so that urgent orders can be met quickly from stock.

**S:** If I placed an order now, how long would it be before I got delivery?

**L:** It would largely depend on the size of the order and the items you want.

**S:** By the way, how large is the factory?

**L:** It covers an area of 50,000 square meters.

**S:** It is much larger than I expected. When was the factory set up?

**L:** In the early 1970's. We will celebrate our 30th anniversary next month.

**S:** Congratulations. How many employees do you have?

**L:** About 200.

## Dialogue 2

*Li Yan and Susan are viewing the showroom.*

**L:** This is our showroom. This way, please.

**S:** I say, you've got some nice things here.

**L:** Yes. Most of our products are very well known all over China, and many of them are manufactured especially to serve our export markets.

**S:** I know you have won a great reputation in the export worldwide.

**L:** You can say that again. The quality of our products is superior and the prices are reasonable.

**S:** That's good. What is this? A laundry basket?

**L:** That's a bamboo laundry basket. Maybe a little austere for foreign tastes.

**S:** I'm afraid it is. What would you say is the trend now in the mood and tastes for this kind of products?

**L:** I'd say there is a gentle move away from the simple to the baroque.

**S:** I share your opinion, but I think the simple styles will remain popular. Odd shapes usually last for a couple of years or so, then give way to something else.

**L:** That's right.

**S:** What kind of quality control do you have?

1. the edge: 优势

**L:** It's extremely tight. Quality is one of our primary considerations.

**S:** That's the way it should be. By the way, do you have any more samples of products?

**L:** Yes, here are the samples.

**S:** Er... They look very good.

# Practice

## Practice 1

Work in pairs and re-introduce the factory with the information in Dialogue 1. The following sentence patterns may be also helpful.

> How large is the plant?
>
> When was the plant set up?
>
> It covers an area of...
>
> We have... employees.
>
> All products go through five checks.

## Practice 2

Suppose you are doing business with an American client in line of white steam filature. Work in pairs, rehearse Dialogue 2 and introduce the product to your partner with the information below. The following words and expressions may be also helpful.

白厂丝 White Steam Filature

规格：20/22D Specification: 20/22D

介绍：本公司主要生产 4A、5A 级优质白厂丝，远销国内外，获得顾客的一致好评。

Introduction: We manly produce quality white steam filature of Grade 4A and 5A, being popular both at home and abroad and well received among the customers.

产品特点：色泽一致,手感好,偏差小,条干均匀,清洁、净度分数高

Characteristics: gentle colour and lustre, fine handle, little windage, equal fiber structure, high cleanness and purity

Would you like to show me...

What is it made of ?

Is it the new model?

How much does it cost?

What about the quality?

How long/wide/high/thick/deep is it?

It is made of iron/porcelain/denim/silk/rayon/fur/linen/bamboo/cotton

## Practice 3

**Pair work**

Mr. Green, the chief manager of an Indian firm, is visiting a Chinese factory which makes men's T-shirts. Mr. Zhang, in charge of the sales department of a large garment factory, is showing him around and giving a brief introduction of their factory. Now you work in pairs to make a dialogue between Mr. Green and Mr. Zhang.

## Practice 4

**Problem–solving:**

As a manager or leader of a factory, the person usually receives guests in a very friendly way and is willing to meet all the guests' demands. However, most factories do not allow the guests to take pictures in the workshops, especially pictures of the production line and the laboratory in case their business secrets will be revealed. Suppose Susan in the Situational Dialogues wants to take pictures of the factory's production process, and you, Li Yan, of course don't allow him to do so. But you know if you reject her requirement directly, she will be unhappy and you're afraid it will lead to the failure of this trade. So in this case, what is the best solution to the problem? Have you got any good ideas? Please share your opinion with your group members and then present it to the whole class.

# *Learning More*

### Factory Safety

The importance of safety and common sense cannot be over stressed. It is reported "Twenty to twenty-five thousand workers in industry within the United States are killed annually while in the course of their employment. Two million suffer non-fatal accidents of varying degree which make them miss days of employment."

Since you cannot possibly teach someone everything, safety is as much common sense as it is preparedness. But continued training, study, and practice build common sense.

Safety means different things to different individuals. Very often one person does not feel safe doing what someone else does all the time. If they do not feel safe doing something, they should stop and call someone to discuss it. They should not do anything that they are not comfortable with.

As employers, you should tell your people to stop and think before they do something. Ask themselves what are the risks and problems that they foresee, and what they can do to minimize risks.

Since factory safety is very critical both to the employers and employees, is it to be wondered at that employers and employees unite in the demand that all involved in industry become active allies in the accident-reduction army?

**Questions for discussion:**

1. How can factory workers build common sense on safety?
2. What should employees do to minimize risks?

# Unit 10

## Making an Inquiry

# Warming Up

What information do you want to obtain before you decide on buying the bamboo baskets in the following pictures?

# Situational Dialogues

## Dialogue 1

*After Li Yan showed her around the factory, Susan was thinking of placing an order with Boyi Arts Trading Company.*

**S:** I'm very glad to have a chance to visit your company. It's so impressive.

**L:** You are always welcome.

**S:** Well, I'm thinking of placing an order with you for some of your basket products. I'm quite sure that these items will find a ready market in France if their prices are found competitive.

**L:** I'm very glad to hear that. What items are you particularly interested in?

**S:** I can't say now. Have you got the latest price lists for these basket products?

**L:** Of course, we have. Here you are. These are price lists for basket products with sample pictures and specifications as well. However, all prices in the lists are subject to our final confirmation.

**S:** Thank you. Are the goods as good as the samples you

display?

**L:** Certainly, I can assure you of our fine quality and reasonable price.

**S:** All right, thank you very much for your patience. I will go into the catalogues and price lists in details, and ring you as soon as I get an idea.

**L:** I'm looking forward to your trial order.

## Dialogue 2

*Several days later, Susan called Li Yan for a specific inquiry for corn baskets.*

**S:** Hello, this is Susan. May I speak to Mr. Li Yan?

**L:** It's me. Good afternoon. What can I do for you?

**S:** Yes. After a careful study of the price lists, we are particularly interested in corn baskets. This product is quite new while the other listed products are already available in European market. Can you quote me your best price for the corn baskets?

**L:** Thanks for your inquiry. Would you tell me the quantity you require so that I can work out our best offer?

**S:** I'm planning to place an order for 2,000 corn baskets to start with.

**L:** OK. Which one would you prefer for the quotation, FOB or CIF?

**S:** I wonder whether you can quote us your CIF price. If your prices are good, I can place the order with you right now.

**L:** I'm sure you will find our price is very competitive, compared with that of the other companies in the same line.

**S:** That's good. When can I have your CIF firm offers for the 2,000 corn baskets?

**L:** We will work out the offer this evening and give it to you tomorrow morning.

**S:** I will be at your office at 10 am tomorrow for the firm offer. Is it all right with you?

**L:** I am willing at your service as always.

# Practice

Practice 1

Student A playing the role of Susan and Student B acting as Li Yan, work in pairs to practise the above situational dialogues with the substitution of the following sentence patterns.

**To show one's interests in certain products**

I would like to know more information about... you advertised in today's China Daily.

We are deeply impressed by the... displayed at your stand at the fair. We would appreciate more details about it.

**Specific enquiry**

I'd like to have your lowest quotations CIF Vancouver for No.... in the category. Can you give us an indication of your price of 5 dozens of... ?

Practice 2

Rearrange the following sentences to make a dialogue. You may add more information to this dialogue.

1. I'm very interested in your bed-covers. Here is a list of requirements. I'd like to have your lowest quotations.

2. I'm very pleased to hear that. I will work out our firm offer, CIF Barcelona for your order tonight.

3. OK. Could you give me an indication of the price?

4. OK. See you tomorrow.

5. In principle, we don't allow any commission. But if your order is large, we will take it into consideration.

6. Thank you for your inquiry. Would you let us know what quantity you require so as to enable us to work out our best quotation.

7. From the price sheets, I find your prices are very competitive. We'd like to place an order of 1,000 pieces. But I would like to have CIF Barcelona price.

8. That will depend on your price. If your price is reasonable and I can get the commission I want, we can place an order immediately.

9. Good. I will come back tomorrow. All right?

10. Here are our latest FOB price sheets. All the prices on the sheets are subject to our final confirmation. When can you decide the size of your order?

Work in pairs to make a dialogue based on the following written enquiry. Student A is enquiring about the Cotton Piece Goods and Student B is replying to the enquiry.

Gentlemen,

We are one of the leading importers of textiles in this city and shall be pleased to establish direct business relations with you.

At present, we are interested in Cotton Piece goods and shall be pleased to receive from you by airmail catalogues, samples and all necessary information regarding these goods so as to acquaint us with the quality and workmanship of your supplies. Meanwhile please quote us your favorable price, C I F San Francisco, inclusive of our 2% commission, stating the earliest date of shipment.

Should your price be found competitive and delivery date acceptable, we intend to place a large order with you.

Truly yours,

## Practice 4

**Presentation**

In a trade enquiry, the enquirer is usually equipped with catalogues and price lists with samples and specifications. Therefore, it's not necessary for them to enquire about the basic facts about the commodity. Suppose you are going to buy  certain products on an Internet shop. Use the library and Internet resources to work out a detailed inquiry for the products you are interested in and set the bottom CIF price that you can accept.

# Learning More

## Inquiry

Inquiry is the request for information about a product or service. An inquiry from a prospective customer may be unsolicited, but many advertising dollars are spent attempting to generate inquiries as well as purchases. Inquiry promotions identify individuals with an interest in the product or service, provide leads for follow-up sales calls or promotions, and measure both the effectiveness of various advertisements and also the demand for a product or service. It is important to answer all inquiries with a follow-up letter or sales call to convert the inquirer to a buyer.

Sales letter sent to someone who has made an inquiry invite the inquirer to make a purchase. This process is generally used for expensive items requiring a lot of information and thought before a purchase decision is made, such as an automobile or an insurance policy. Follow-up letters differ from other promotional mailings in that they are mailed in response to an inquiry on an individual basis in contrast to being mailed in bulk on a date determined by the mailer. The first follow-up letter in a series is usually the most detailed, while subsequent efforts highlight individual benefits.

**Questions for Discussion:**

1. How does advertising help to bring up the prospect?
2. How do the follow-up letters convert the inquirer into a buyer?

# Unit 11

# Making an Offer

# Warming Up

1. What's the main difference between offers with engagement and offers without engagement and why is it important to remind the enquirer of the validity of an offer?
2. Do you know the meaning of these terms and the differences between them?

**trade discount**

**quantity discount**

**cash discount**

**loyalty discount**

# Situational Dialogues

### Dialogue 1

*Next day, Susan came to Li Yan's office.*

**L:** Good morning, Susan.

**S:** Good morning, Mr. Li. Did you finally figure out the quotation?

**L:** Yes, I'd like to quote you USD 1.58 per piece CIF European main ports, payment to be made by L/C.

**S:** Well, the price is much higher than what I have expected. Chinese basket products are well sold in French market. The main reason is that the price is very favorable.

**L:** That's true. The prices of our hand-made corn products are much lower than that of those from other sources and our quality is also much superior.

**S:** You said it.  Could you give me a discount as this is a general practice?

**L:** We do offer 10% discount for an order of more than 5,000 pieces.

**S:** 5,000 pieces! You see, this is only our trial order. And if the first lot of the goods is good and well sold,  we'd like to repeat the order and have regular orders.

**L:** I highly appreciate it.  But I'm sorry we couldn't make a change to the settled-price principle of the corporation.

**S:** Thank you for your offer.  I will talk to my general manager to see if it is possible to increase the quantity to get the discount.

**L:** I'm very grateful to you for your efforts.

**S:** By the way, is the offer a firm one?

**L:** Yes. The validity is 4 days. That remains open until 5:00 pm, this Friday, our time.

**S:** Fine, thank you. I will ring you as soon as possible.

## Dialogue 2

*Susan is negotiating with Li Yan to settle the quotation over the phone.*

**S:** Mr. Li, I've talked to my general manager and he has agreed to increase the number to 5,000 pieces but we ask for a 20% quantity discount.

**L:** I do appreciate the effort you're making towards reaching an agreement.  But 20% is far more than we can offer to any of our customers.

**S:** Your prices are higher than we have from elsewhere taking such a large quantity into account.

**L:** But you should take the quality into consideration.  You know our products are of high quality and well known all over the world.  You will be assured of efficient service for years to come.

**S:** The labor cost has decreased a lot recently, however. I think you can reduce the price accordingly.

**L:** I appreciate your counter-offer. But it's beyond our reach.

**S:** Maybe we can go half way to meet each other.  How about 15%?

1. the edge: 优势

**L:** Maybe we can accept the 15% quantity discount for an initial order. But I have to consult my manager for sure.

**S:** OK, I trust through our mutual cooperation, substantial transactions can be concluded between us.

# Practice

## Practice 1

Student A playing the role of Susan and Student B acting as Li Yan, work in pairs to practise the above situational dialogues with the substitution of the following sentence patterns.

**Offer**

Our price is US $... per set CIF Aden including your commission of 2%.

The price is subject to a 20% trade discount off net price.

US$... is our rock bottom price.

**Counter–Offer**

As we usually place very large orders, we would expect a quantity discount in addition to the trade discount you offer.

As we intend to place regular orders, we wonder if you could give us a 20% quantity discount.

**Rejection**

Because we work on a fast turnover and small profit margins basis, we do not offer any trade discount.

It would be uneconomical for us to offer our products at the discount you suggest.

**As to the validity of the offer**

Our offer will stay effective for 7 days.

Our offer remains unchanged until 5pm, this Friday, our time.

## Practice 2

Rearrange the following sentences to make a dialogue. You may add more information to this dialogue.

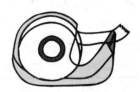

1. OK.
2. I should consult my manager. How long will this offer

be open?

3. I've compared your quotation with the prevailing market prices and with that of other suppliers', and I find your price is really high.

4. I think you will agree that our products are of the best quality compared with the similar products in the world. Besides they are brightly colored and beautifully patterned.

5. It will remain open for 3 days.

6. I'd like to talk with you about the price you quoted last week on bed-covers.

7. I agree. But you know, no product, however attractive, will sell well if it's too expensive.

8. Well, then, what is the price you would say?

9. But this is the best quotation we can make. We consider it a rock-bottom price indeed.

10. That's really beyond my means. Taking the large quantity into account, let's meet each other half way at US $8 per piece.

11. The best we can accept is US $5 per piece.

12. I'm sorry to hear that. But we still find no way to accept your quotation.

## Practice 3

Mr. Smith (played by student A), who is a businessman from Austria, is trying to buy 1, 000 laser printers from Tony (played by Student B), sales representative of Shanghai No. 1 Electronics Corporation. They are conducting a tedious negotiation about the price. On the part of the offering party, Tony is trying to convince Mr. Smith that his offer of AUS$ 100 each is the best, while on the part of the inquiring party, Mr. Smith tries every means to persuade Tony to lower down the price to AUS$ 70 each.

## Practice 4

Suppose you have opened a shop on the Internet. Use the library or the Internet resources to look for some products you are willing to sell in your shop. Offer the price for each product and say what contribute to your offer.

# Learning More

### Offer

An offer is a communication that gives the listener the power to conclude a contract. The question of whether a party in fact made an offer is a common question in a contract case. The general rule is that it must be reasonable under the circumstances for the recipient to believe that the communication is an offer. The more definite the communication, the more likely it is to constitute an offer. If an offer spells out such terms as quantity, quality, price, and time and place of delivery, a court may find that an offer was made. For example, if a merchant says to a customer, "I will sell you a dozen high-grade widgets for $100 each to be delivered to your shop on December 31.", a court would likely find such a communication sufficiently definite to constitute an offer. On the other hand, a statement such as "I am thinking of selling some widgets" would probably not be labeled an offer.

If an offer indicates that it will terminate within a certain period of time, it cannot be accepted after the time has expired. The passage of a reasonable length of time may automatically terminate an offer. The determination of a reasonable length of time depends on the circumstances surrounding the offer. For example, if a wholesaler contacts a retailer offering to sell perishable produce, the retailer cannot wait six weeks and then accept the offer. Even if an item is nonperishable, an unusually lengthy response time may terminate an offer. For example, if the usual practice in the lumber business is a response time of less than two weeks, the offerer may refuse to honor the offer if the recipient of the offer does not respond within that time period.

**Questions for Discussion:**
1. What contributes to the constitution of an offer?
2. Why is the validity of an offer necessary?

# Unit 12

## Price Reduction

# Warming Up

"Alright, follow my lead. I'll call it 'just a dog box',
then you say, 'but there's not even a run'."
Maybe we can get the price down to 200."

1.  In daily life, you may do lots of shopping. Do you tend to bargain? What strategies may you use to ask for a price reduction?
2.  Suppose you are a keeper of a boutique, how could you sell your clothes while sticking to a favorable price?

# Situational Dialogues

## Dialogue 1

*After consulting, Li Yan is talking with Susan again about the price.*

**S:** Mr. Li, we are very satisfied with the efforts you have made to conclude the business between us. Now shall we have the final price for your corn baskets? We would expect a bigger quantity discount.

**L:** I'm quite pleased to hear that, but you see 10% quantity discount has already been reduced to the limit.

**S:** But this time we are placing a big order.

**L:** The fact is that at present many orders pour in at a higher price. So we can't make reduction of the price.

S: If that's the case, there is hardly any need for further discussion. We might as well call the whole deal off.

L: Well, in order to establish the business relations with you, we can grant you a special discount of another 3%. It's the best we can do.

S: A 13% discount? That doesn't make a difference. You know we usually deal on a 20% quantity discount for such large orders.

L: It would be uneconomical for us to offer our products at the discount you suggest.

S: Your concession will set the ball rolling. Let us settle it at a total discount of 15%, if you agree.

L: I have consulted my manager and we can not do that for an order of 5,000. Maybe you can consider increasing the quantity to 10,000, and then we can offer you the discount you desire.

## Dialogue 2

*Li yan is now persuading susan to accept the proposal for placing an order of 10,000.*

S: 10,000 is more than we can handle. You see it is a trial order, and we have no confidence in the market.

L: You have no need to worry about market. According to our market prediction, the demand is quite large and will exceed supply in near future. As our corn baskets are of fine quality, customers in other countries would like to place orders with us even if some other sources offer similar kinds at much lower prices.

S: We do not deny the quality of your products is slightly better, but the current price you offer is really difficult for us to push the sales in our more competitive market.

L: It is the quality that really counts. I think you agree that for the same quality, there is nowhere else you get the same price.

S: Can't you see your way to reduce the price by another 5% for the same quantity?

L: I'm afraid 13% discount is already our best offer for 5,000 pieces.

**S:** In order to get the business, we are willing to make some concessions. 15% for 10,000 pieces.

**L:** Great. Let's call it a deal. USD 1.34 per piece for 10,000 pieces corn baskets.

**S:** OK. I hope we both can get something out of this.

# Practice

## Practice 1

Student A playing the role of Susan and Student B acting as Li Yan, work in pairs to practise the above situational dialogues with the substitution of the following sentence patterns.

**Asking for price reduction**

Your price is too high for us to accept.

If you insist on your price, we can hardly come to terms.

**Making a compromise**

With an eye to future business, we agree to grant you a 1 % discount.

May I suggest that we go fifty—fifty and close the gap.

We'd like to make a concession to 20% discount.

## Practice 2

Rearrange the following sentences to make a dialogue.

You may add more information to this dialogue.

1. Have you brought the fax with you?

2. $24.00 per watch.

3. Here you are.

4. As the market is soaring, we suggest you accept our price as soon as possible.

5. You see, we want very much to distribute your watches in our region. Anyhow, your price should be more competitive.

6. I'm afraid not. You may be aware that the market of these watches is soaring.

7. What a pity! Then what's your price now?

8. Yes, it's the fax we sent you last month. But the price was only valid till the end of last month.

9. No, I'm sorry we can't. I am sure the goods will be readily saleable in your market at this price.

10. I want to buy your electronic watches at the price you quoted in your fax.

11. Our price is in fact more advantageous than other suppliers'.

12. Well, to let you start the business in your market, we can give you a 2% discount.

13. Can you allow a 6% discount?

14. Can we still conclude business at this price?

15. I need to consider it more carefully. And then I'll get back to you.

16. Why, your price has gone up too much. It's 10% higher than the price quoted in your fax. It would be difficult for us to make any sales at such a price.

## Practice 3

Simon is the sales manger of COMPAQ, he offers US $950 per set of computer to Steve, a distributor based on their good relations. Steve expects the price to be reduced to US$800 per set. Simon can't satisfy this counter-offer but he may reduce the price by 2%, i.e. $931 per set and he insists it is their rock-bottom price.

Work in pairs and play the roles of Simon and Steve and make a dialogue by adding your respective strategies to negotiate the price.

## Practice 4

A careful plan before the price negotiation is indispensable and important. Use the library or the Internet resources to search for the factors you need to take into consideration in the plan on the part of both parties as the seller and buyer.

TEAMWORK TAKES PLANNING

# Learning More

### Price Negotiation

At the negotiating table, the price is usually the key point. In order to achieve a favorable outcome from the negotiation, the following points should be paid attention to:

Making a higher offer at the beginning of negotiation

If you are an exporter, you should make a high offer at the beginning of the negotiation and try you best to achieve your best aim through negotiation. Reducing your prices step by step will make a good impression on the other party, he will be pleased to cooperate with you. And on this situation, he may well accept your quotation as the best price.

Making no compromise in the matter of prices at the beginning of negotiations

If you are an exporter, remember never to make compromise in the matter of prices at the beginning of negotiations, or you will lose other advantages, such as the product's quality, the firm's experience and credit, and other conditions of transaction being of benefit to you.

Rejecting an exporter's price at the outset of the negotiation

As an importer, you should reject the exporter's price at the outset of the discussion in order to get the upper hand from the start of negotiation, thereby hoping to obtain maximum concessions on other matters. At least, you may force your counterpart to cut down the high price he offers.

Making no concession on price at once when the importer doesn't accept the offer

If the price quoted by the exporter has not been accepted by importer, the exporter should react positively by initiating on non-price questions, instead of immediately offering price concessions or taking defensive attitude. Only by knowing the causes of the importer's disapproving the offer can an exporter make a new offer acceptable to importer or make other arrangements.

**Question for Discussion:**

1. What are the principles that the exporter and importer should pay attention to respectively?

2. Besides the favorable prices, what are the other advantage a seller can add to the attraction of the deal?